Watch The Doors As They Close

Karen Lillis

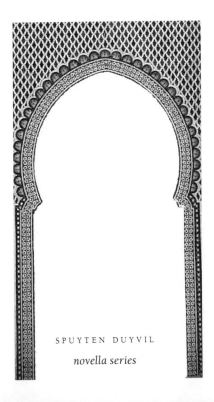

SPUYTEN DUYVIL

novella series

ACKNOWLEDGEMENTS

First I want to thank Nava Renek and Tod Thilleman for taking on this book. I am thrilled to be in the company of the exciting literature, radical writers, and intelligent authors whom Spuyten Duyvil publishes in such beautiful editions.

The next round of thanks goes to the readers of the earliest draft of this novella, whose immediate enthusiasm for the story led me to seek publication. Huge appreciation goes out to Margarita Shalina, Amy George Brown, James Chapman, Angela Diehl, Elsa LiDonni, Filip Marinovich, Beth Megas, Roberta Retacchi, Noel Salzman, and Geoffrey Cruickshank-Hagenbuckle. I am grateful to Andrea Hiott and the other editors at Pulse Berlin, and Lynn Alexander and Doug Mathewson at Blink Ink, for publishing outtakes of the book; I thank Wednesday Kennedy and Michael Kimball for their warm encouragement of the book after reading outtakes. I am deeply grateful for the readers who gave feedback on my revisions: Jessica Fenlon, Scott McClanahan, John Megas, and Michelle Reale. I send heartfelt thanks to Lori Jakiela and Christen Clifford for inviting me to perform the first two public readings from this book. I am thrilled that the talented photographer Camille Lacroix has allowed me to use his beautiful image for the book cover.

Finally, I am hugely grateful to Thomas for his patience, generosity, and care in reading multiple drafts of the novel. He has provided invaluable support to me in the form of intelligent overviews, suggestions, and corrections as well as much enthusiasm for the success of the book.

ISBN 978-0-923389-87-1

Library of Congress Cataloging-in-Publication Data

Lillis, Karen E., 1970-
Watch the doors as they close / Karen Lillis.
p. cm.
ISBN 978-0-923389-87-1
1. Bookstores--Employees--Fiction. 2. Reminiscing--Fiction. 3. Brooklyn (New York, N.Y.)--Fiction. I. Title.
PS3612.I425W38 2012
813'.6--dc23
2011050170

For Geoffrey Cruickshank-Hagenbuckle

WATCH THE DOORS AS THEY CLOSE

This is the story of Anselm. The story of Anselm as told to me. Anselm gave me this beautiful book as a present for no reason (for love) in late September or early October. He told me he was giving me this journal because I'm the first writer he'd ever met who had something to say. (I was even more flattered by this boast when it came out that he'd slept with all the female poets at Yaddo one summer during a manic phase.)

Anselm bought this book in Paris in November 1997, when we each happened to be in Paris. I was there in my second month (of two) and he was there for three or four weeks in November. He was there on a commission from _____?, writing music. They sent him two plane tickets and put him up in a two or three star hotel in the cinquième district—he was living on the street that passes Café Panis, perpendicular to the Seine. He was living right near Shakespeare and Company and Bistro des Artistes, and I was hanging around the same area during that time; I think Raymond got there in the last week of October or so. I wasn't living at Shakespeare anymore by then but I'd meet Raymond there, I remember him buying me an omelette lunch at Panis and how grateful I was. Also Julia lived on that street, a bit farther down away from the Seine. I spent time with her in her little attic apartment (the upstairs maid's quarters), both of us lamenting the rainy season and so much grey.

Anselm was given two plane tickets to Paris, and by the time he was going, he really wanted to take Meredith, the Scorpio-with-Scorpio-rising poet he was screwing then (while her boyfriend was living in another city and Anselm and Meredith were telling everyone they were working on an opera together). But he found that the ticket was non-transferable, and as it was in his then ex-girlfriend April's name, he "had" to take her. So they lived parallel lives in Paris for a month. He'd write during the day (in the hotel room? or maybe in cafés, Anselm always wrote in cafés or bars in New York, the white noise helped him write music because he could concentrate on hearing the noises in his head and then recording them. He always had sounds in his head; that was the musician in him) and April would cavort around Paris on her own. I think the only other story I know about them in Paris was that he was out at a club one night and met a Swedish or Scandinavian woman named Anna or Anika, and they got drunk and took a whole roll of "compromising pictures" on Anselm's camera. But the film got mixed up with April's by accident, so she saw the pictures and he never did. She was, of course, livid.

Meredith was the woman that Anselm was cheating on April with, after she (April) wouldn't accept their breakup. April was psychotic, a Scorpio also, and wouldn't accept that Anselm truly wanted it to be over. She was such a headstrong brat (probably 20 or 21 by then) that she thought she could ignore the breakup and get away with it. Anselm was never the cheating kind, this I believe, but he felt so voiceless that April wouldn't listen to him; it made him want to leave her. She hadn't acknowledged HIM in a long time, OR he had started "playing dead" for her—capitulating to her wishes. He said by the end of their relationship things had deteriorated to the point that he would go to her place and screw her until *she* had an orgasm, then leave. Do his duty because that's what she expected of him. She never accepted *his* moods, or the rhythm of *his* sexuality—she wanted to have sex when *she* wanted and that was that.

When Anselm gets depressed, his libido is out the window. He can't feel any emotions, only anxiety about not feeling any emotion. He doesn't often remember these blocks of time. Sometimes they last a few hours, sometimes days, sometimes months. He calls it "the bad space." When he starts going there he starts getting shaky and scared. Anxious. The shaky feels like after you've been crying for a long, long time. When he's in the bad space he is almost absent to himself (though he seems to sit with it and try to cope with the accompanying anxiety—other times he just wants to be distracted, like watching movies—still other times he can't bear it and he drinks to take the edge off) but he can seem strangely present to the person he's with. Still, he'll probably lose the memory of most of your time spent, so don't be offended.

I'm not actually positive that it was Meredith that Anselm cheated with, I've just put it together from context clues. So the final breakup with April eventually went that Anselm told her about his new lover—he thought she had figured it out by that point but apparently her self-involvement (vain ego?) prevented her from recognizing the signs. So he clued her in and emphasized it with "Why do you think I've been out EVERY SINGLE NIGHT?"

Meredith, in any case, was supposed to be a casual affair. Or at least it was supposed to be from Meredith's point of view. She wasn't planning to leave her boyfriend. But Anselm was really starting to like her and wanted to know what the story was—who were they? How did she feel? She was evasive about it, a jerk to him.

Eventually, Meredith's boyfriend came back to town for a visit. The three of them ended up at the same bar. The boyfriend, who knew Anselm, and knew that Anselm and Meredith were friends, noticed that they weren't speaking. Finally came over to say hi to Anselm and ask him what was up. Anselm said, "Do you want the truth or do you want the diplomatic version?" The boyfriend wanted to know what that meant—and claimed that he wanted the truth. Anselm reported, with all the force of his anger towards Meredith: "Your girlfriend and I have been sleeping together for the last six weeks." The boyfriend was shocked to hear these words and wouldn't, couldn't believe them. Anselm was in a fury; he was on a roll. "You don't believe me? What do you want me to tell you? What she says when she comes, her fascination with hip bones, the mole on her inner thigh?" This, I believe, was when Meredith stopped talking to Anselm for good. Anselm was also shunned by most of the Oberlin poets, Meredith's friends, after that.

Anselm told me that story the day after he read my novel—the same day he told me how jealous and angry the Polish boyfriend chapter made him. (Inexplicably, he said. He very rarely gets jealous.) So I felt that the Meredith story was told in retaliation. It came across the phone lines (Anselm was in Pennsylvania; I was on the diner pay phone in Brooklyn) like a vindictive tell-all. I almost felt I deserved it since he had to hear about my braggart tales via my novel (still unsure about the how and why of my own tell-all), but in any case I got sick with jealousy for about two days. Poisoned my love with anxiety, with blackest self-doubt. I was on such a high right before that.

So, this book. Anselm bought this book with the idea of giving it to someone one day, but he wasn't sure who. He just thought it was beautiful. Luxurious. Thick, cream-colored pages with deckled edges and pockmarked leather cover. He gave it to me while we were sitting on my futon-as-a-couch in my bedroom, after I got home from work one night. He presented it with such earnest loving.

13 December 2003

This journal is about Anselm Vaughn Brkich-David, now Anselm Vaughn Brkić, born Anselm Vaughn David in the Western Pennsylvania town of Bald Hill at 3:24 a.m. on June 25, 1972. He was born to Peggy Brkich David and Vaughn David. They lived in Bobtown, Pennsylvania at some point early on, maybe when he was born. They soon came to inhabit the family homestead, maybe after a grandparent fell ill or maybe after Anselm's younger sister (Leeanne) was born. They lived in this house for many years, although eventually his mother sold it, needing the money, and it now stands in disrepair. She lives today in an apartment in Waynesburg, Pennsylvania. All of this is in the same county in Appalachia.

Things Anselm hates: Mozart; short hair ("God didn't mean for anyone to keep cutting what grows fine on its own"); watching anyone else have fun when he's in THAT MOOD; being put in a group of people, especially in private quarters; families; holidays; women who are taller than him; his mother; anchovies; being tickled, or anything that tickles; sneakers; the color pink.

14 December 2003

Anselm hates raw onions because the texture reminds him of (or is it the look of them?) tapeworms he remembers stepping on, on his grandfather's farm. There would be all these slaughtered animal parts around and the tapeworms would emerge out of the entrails—or was it that the tapeworms would crawl out of the live animals and just be laying around? No, I think the former. I don't know how farms work. I don't know why slaughtered animal parts would be laying on the ground, something like they slopped the pigs with the stuff, but I'm sure they had a trough for that. This was the same grandfather, I believe, who periodically rounded up all the unwanted kittens on the farm and threw them together in a ruck sack, drove to the river and drowned them by tossing the whole sack in. "I'm sleeping with a kitten killer?" I asked Anselm in pissed-offness when he told me. "No, my grandfather did it, I just accompanied him sometimes," Anselm said. I suppose in Appalachia it was considered the humane thing to do.

I think I only ever heard of one grandfather. His mother's father. A Croatian, he must have been a Croatian immigrant. Anselm grew up speaking Croatian with his mother until he was seven years old. (He also grew up with a thick Appalachian accent, then made a concerted effort to learn standard American English—when?—in college, I guess. Undergrad. Surrounded by the post-New England preppies of Oberlin.) His grandfather's brother, they all found out very late, was a high-ranking officer in the Croatian Army, the Ustasi, which was in bed with the Third Reich. But his grandfather hadn't spoken to his brother in years. The Croatian immigrant had married a Ukrainian who was a few generations in, and Anselm's grandmother was Russian Orthodox; his mother had raised Anselm and Leeanne as such. The fasts and the feasts and the all-day masses. Anselm says that vomiting reminds him of religious holidays because everyone's been fasting for days and then they gorge in celebration. Advent and Lent sounded especially brutal.

I remember being on the payphone on Nassau Avenue at 11:00 p.m. or so, talking to Anselm in Pennsylvania (this would have been in August), and laughing and admitting that I thought that his being raised Orthodox was really sexy. Then I told him that Irina had described a Russian Orthodox wedding to me, all the ornamentation and the crowns and everything, and I laughed again and told him if I saw a video of that it would be like watching porn. Anselm was like, "Well, there'll be no Orthodox weddings in my life, sorry to disappoint...." I said, no, I didn't mean I needed to *have* an Orthodox wedding, I just wanted to *see* one.

Anselm had embraced his religion as a young adult, maybe after he'd originally rejected it—and during this embrace he was studious and devout—so he knew everything I could ever want to ask him about the religion. I didn't even know enough to know what questions to ask. I remember a conversation about Orthodox saints; I asked him what his saint's name was, and he said he didn't have one. He said they have different saints entirely, and anyway they don't do that. I was skeptical.

Anselm eventually rejected Orthodoxy again, even though I think he said he went as far as contemplating being a priest. He definitely told me that he thought about becoming a monk when he went to Austria. He visited a mountain there that's the home of a monastery; only men are allowed to set foot on the mountain.

Austria is Anselm's favorite place in the world, he wants to grow old and die there. Preferably staring into the Danube, a little downstream from Vienna.

That's how he talks sometimes—other times he claims that he should have died in the summer of 1999. That he's already dead, and he's just waiting for the rest of himself to notice. That—how did he put it?—he's living on borrowed time. "I don't expect anything out of my life," he'd always say. "And I used to."

That grandfather (I don't know what his pet name for him was, what they called him) was a hard worker. I think Anselm said he worked on the farm every day of his life, up until he got sick. It was a tumor, I think. He spent the last nine months of his life in the hospital with a jumble of tubes feeding into his limbs. Anselm and his sister would go and visit him and he was so embarrassed to be seen in this state after being so able-bodied. I don't remember why he had all the tubes, if it was to send food or medicine through his blood, if he couldn't eat through his mouth or he just needed extra fluids in his veins, but Anselm showed me a picture of him from then, he looked sweet and sad. Sitting up in the angled hospital bed, in a white paper robe. In front of a white wall, pale face. Everything washed-out white. Trying to smile, if I remember. The photo looked like from the '80s. Rounded corners, slightly out of focus, as if from low batteries on an auto focus camera.

His grandmother didn't, of course, remarry.

Anselm hated birds, boxer shorts, mornings, ham, girly girls, ballet, the smell of mint, humidity, cold, dead repetition in music, dishonesty, and turkey. He loved bodies of water, but especially rivers. He could sit and look at a river for hours. Rivers and their motion seemed to contain the whole universe for him.

Anselm was the first drinker I ever was in love with (Josh was Straight Edge, Steven had gone dry for me, and Conor—due to the fact that he was allergic to grains, and Ireland being the home of whiskey and beer—had never had a drink in his life) and I was the first non-drinker he'd ever dated. Not that I'm a complete tee-totaller. I met him when I was shit-faced drunk, let's see, how many drinks was I into it? I was drinking vodka and cokes that night, though when I met Anselm (at 2:00 a.m.) I liked him enough that I wanted to sober up, so when he offered to buy me a drink, I let him get me a seltzer. They gave it to me in a pint glass that had a slight curve to its shape, and topped it with a lemon and I drank it from the straw they gave me. I remember the glass seeming just huge, and I felt a little silly or maybe just girly, like I was on a 1950s date sipping a malted at the counter at Schraft's. Maybe that's because I was so happy for Anselm's concerted attention, or should I say, a vivacious stranger's.

Later Anselm would get nervous when I drank vodka; he said he's sworn off combining women and vodka. The women he knew drank vodka, and the vodka made them mean—I think he meant Sandra, Catherine, Meredith, and April, but I guess Sandra's the only one I'm sure about. She got really mean—a belligerent, argumentative drunk—with a few vodkas in her, and apparently she never stopped at a few. Other times it was beer they shared. He'd go hang out with her at her studio in the artists' building that's been there forever on Kent Avenue, and they'd pick up a case of beer and finish it off. Anselm said that they'd ended the relationship by coming to a mature, mutual decision (neither was in love) that they weren't right for each other romantically, after which they proceeded to be very good friends. Anselm said once that she was probably the person he trusted the most in New York, although later he didn't seem to feel that way. He also told me, in a separate conversation, that Sandra and he had an understanding as "friends," that they slept together sometimes, no strings attached. I remember Anselm using the phrase "whenever we got antsy."

This seems at once incredibly cathartic to write and also may be bringing up an incredible amount of rage I have towards Anselm. I've been writing this story in my head all day, walking to the subway and at work (I'm at lunch now) but I've also been incredibly hyper all day to-day—high energy, boiling anger somewhere in my belly, on the verge of snapping any minute.

Anselm and I broke up a week ago—a week ago, today, in fact. On the phone, after he'd already left New York again to return to his mother's house in Pennsylvania. Waynesburg. See, Anselm and I met right before he was about to leave New York indefinitely. We met on a Friday night, and he didn't know that then. But by the time we communicated the Wednesday after, he was planning to go to Pennsylvania for three or four months—most directly because his grandmother (his mother's mother) had just died. Besides which, his job had just dried up, he'd just put in for taking a year off school, and his lease had ended. And he was exhausted from the previous school-year, he'd pretty much had it with New York for awhile.

Our first meeting was so intense that we both wanted to meet again before he left. Our second date was less than 24 hours before he would leave the city by Greyhound the next morning. After I committed to the thought of him (I didn't at first, my usual early-on fickleness), I never doubt-ed that we'd end up together. So by the end of that second, afternoon date, we were saying goodbye at the First Avenue subway station and Anselm was saying, "Two weeks! Okay, I'll come back in two weeks!" (I didn't believe him, I wasn't sure why he was saying it.) As it turned out, he came back about six weeks later, on a bus again, on September 11th. Moved in with me, though neither of us meant it to be that, and stayed for almost three months. He left again, after a lot of love and a lot of tears had passed, on the day after Thanksgiving.

But I was telling you about Sandra. Sandra was the last relationship Anselm had before me, unless you count Erin, though I don't, and he met all three of us at Sophie's on 5th Street. Sandra and Anselm were both living on East 7th when they met. She fell into his "Mrs. Robinson fetish" category (my term), though he never did let it slip how old she was. He was sleeping on her couch the last few days of his stay in New York, and we dropped by there on our second date for Anselm to change his shirt. (He was sweaty from running all the way from Chelsea to the East Village to meet me.) I saw a picture of her then, from a wedding party she was in. Pink bridesmaid dress, she was cute but in a boring Midwestern way: hair short but no style, medium brown, everything about her, medium brown. She was from one of the I states, Illinois or Indiana or Iowa. Divorced from a Russian man, a playwright or an actor. She was in Mensa, I used to love it when Anselm would drop that so casually in his stories about her, it cracked me up. When I say I loved it, I mean I hated it, who the fuck still cares about Mensa? Either way it totally cracks me up, the fact that anyone cares about the Mensa Society or about qualifying "genius" by some number cracks me up.

Sandra (Cassandra was her whole name) programmed databases for a living. Or was it that she was trying to break into that business and it's really hard to? She also taught computer art at three colleges in the tri-state area, she had a car. Kean and Stevens Institute in New Jersey, and one of the closer SUNY's—was it Stony Brook? I don't think it was New Paltz or Purchase. Her own art was a several-step process, something like making paintings of these architectural-figure objects and then making them into computer animation and then into architectural models? No, I think it was the other way round. They were computer models first, figured out in there in whatever math or design the computer is capable of; then she'd paint them from the computer image. I don't remember anymore where the architectural models came into it—I just remember Anselm saying that he felt the architectural aspects were the more philosophically interesting end of her work, but that she was more interested in pushing it into animation. He showed me something on the wall in the "studio" in her place which he then narrated—a painting of the computer-rendered figures—a family sitting down to dinner? They had square bodies, and the background was plaid. It looked hideous and uninteresting, but who am I to judge in-progress art by someone I don't know? There was some extended storyline about a talking caterpillar and a mad bartender who'd poisoned people.

What else do I know about Sandra? It sounded like she was in her late 40s, at least. She was a Taurus, one of the very few non-Scorpios Anselm ever dated. They were together on Sandra's birthday; Anselm told me he had the idea to write a piece of music for her birthday gift, but a few days later he realized she was "just a drunk" and he was never going to fall in love with her, so he didn't. I thought about this story on my birthday, when Anselm and I spent the entire day together but Anselm didn't do squat to celebrate it. I mean no card, no letter, no sex, no make-out session. There was a half-hearted "happy birthday" toast at the dinner I was paying for. And there was the promise that if he had money, he'd have taken me to the Casa de la Femme on West Broadway, an Egyptian restaurant that would have cost him four or five hundred dollars for the meal. Anselm was good at promises. I was good at hoping for the future, hoping and waiting for his promises to come true.

I think Sandra was bisexual. Almost all of Anselm's girlfriends were—Anselm used to say that April was the one totally straight girlfriend he'd had. I think I remember a story about a huge party at the Triangle Building on West 14th Street and Ninth Avenue. Sandra and her friend Dennis and Anselm, and the rest of her friends were all her lesbian pals, and they were all dead drunk, and Anselm and Sandra got into a huge fight as she was getting into a cab with all of her entourage, and Anselm ended up passing out on a sidewalk on 14th Street and spending the night there. I think that story was told to me as an example of how Anselm doesn't pass out from alcohol very often. Or even get drunk. I've seen him put away twelve pints of Guinness and call himself not-drunk. And in fact he doesn't "seem" drunk, usually.

The other image I have of Anselm and Sandra is of her calling him up after she received a delivery of organic foods from "Fresh Direct" and telling him to come over and cook something for her. He'd do this all the time, even though he was not interested in eating the food he'd cooked. This was another example of this sort of curious "dutiful son" role he played for the women in his life—I thought of this as a less extreme version of the way he "serviced" Catherine and April in bed. Or maybe I'm wrong, maybe it was the opposite. Cavorting with yuppies like Sandra gave him the chance to cook and be a food snob on someone else's dime.

He did love cooking, though, maybe I'm being too nasty to call it part of his masochism or his mooching. He once said that cooking was his only real remaining hobby; every other talent he had he'd either stopped pursuing (like playing music) or was pursuing as a career or vocation (writing music, writing poetry). He had even cooked a few times in St. Petersburg, at an old, old restaurant, I think on the Gulf side. It had a name very similar to a very famous restaurant. I think the famous one was Ponce de Leon, and Anselm's restaurant was Fuente Ponce de Leon, some extra word. His place was respected and known locally;

the other one was in all of the guidebooks, etc. He was a sous chef or a line cook for them. It sounded like he'd only lived in St. Petersburg for brief periods of time, like maybe over two or three month-long Winter Breaks during his Bachelor's at Oberlin. The central Ohio winters were too brutal to endure if you didn't have to. The wind hurling itself with all its might across the lake and the flat, flat land, with nothing in the way to say otherwise. Still he was impressed with the East Coast winds, the way they picked up so much character and angles rising in swells up hills and through valleys and past trees and such. I remember him commenting on this to the innkeeper when we went up to the Hudson Valley for my birthday. I remember that day—the wind!—they'd called for amazing winds, and they weren't wrong. I woke up and heard them. I lay in bed for an hour not even ready to open my eyes but just listening to these amazing gale force winds with such excitement. It was the Wind of Change! I wanted to go somewhere and catch it, see what it meant. I told Anselm when we woke up much later, "We're either going to Coney Island, or the Hudson Valley, or to a really tall hotel in Midtown." I asked him if he had any preference, any ideas, but he kept putting it off on me. "It's *your* birthday." My mother had sent me a check and I was determined to get out of town for 24 hours at least. It's not as easy to get out of New York City as it might seem. I mean, we've got Greyhound, Amtrak, New Jersey Transit, Long Island Railroad, Metro North, Grand Central, Penn Station, Port Authority, LaGuardia and JFK, but it takes a reason to get out of town. It takes money, a place to go, motivation, remembering that there is something outside New York City. And of course time. Or energy. Whichever comes first. Weekends in New York are not really time; they're just the space where you recharge yourself before you go back to work again. (I finally did some laundry about two months after Anselm moved in. Although, come to think of it, he never went and did his. Just a few handwashings of socks and underwear. Probably some shirts.)

The Wind of Change? The signs were there for the reading, but I didn't want to: Mainly, I was thoroughly disappointed by his lack of ceremony over my birthday. I just wanted some sign that he thought I was special, that I was someone special in his life, that he loved me (he didn't even say that on that day), hell, that he was still in the relationship. And yet I'd made sure that I was immune to disappointment. I didn't want THAT day to be tainted with such a thing, so I decided in advance that I would Expect Nothing. But no one should expect so much nothing from their lover on their birthday, and if they get it, that tells them everything they need to know.

Maybe I told myself on that day, "I don't even know the guy, maybe he doesn't celebrate birthdays. Maybe birthdays traumatize him, too." Because he told me that his mother hadn't given him a birthday present since he was thirteen. He said he didn't really care about celebrating his own birthday, except that he liked to keep up a tradition he'd inadvertently started of being in a different city for every year. I think age eleven was the first year that he started, that was with a trip with choir.

Now, I think I may be mixing up a few stories, or maybe I'm just putting together stories that were told to me about the same trip at different times. But if I'm correct, then age 18 was the trip to D.C. where Anselm saw black people for the first time, and also the trip during which his sister (back home) got caught giving a blow job to some older guy under the bleachers at the football game. Anselm's mother blamed him for it anyway. "Everything was MY FAULT according to her," he'd say.

There were no family vacation stories from Anselm, but he did go on many trips. There were trips with his music teacher's church choir, like the one to small-town Ohio where the boys who stayed with the parish priest got maybe-molested but wouldn't talk about it; there were Boy Scout trips, like the one to ____? Dakota when it was so cold they almost froze to death, or the one to I-don't-re-member-maybe-West-Virginia to a big Boy Scout camping grounds. Anselm's troop leader played a trick on him, act-ing like they desperately needed some certain thing or else they wouldn't be able to set up camp, and the thing was a nonsense word like, "Anselm, go get us a Right-Handed Intrepid Carbuncle—as fast as you can!" He was to go to camp headquarters, which was three miles away, and it happened to be pouring rain. The thing was, it wasn't just a trick—it was *the* trick that Boy Scout leaders always played on unsuspecting scouts. So the guys at headquarters knew the game. When Anselm got there and approached the two men behind the desk (I pictured it like a hotel desk without the hotel) and asked for "a right-handed intrepid carbuncle," one guy cracked up completely and the other guy kept his composure enough to say: "A right-handed intrepid carbuncle? Why, I have only a left-handed one at the moment." Anselm didn't know what to do. They went back and forth about whether he should just check out a left-handed one instead, but in the end, the desk clerk convinced him that he might really need a right-handed one if his troop leader thought so, and he should go back to the camp and find out. Three miles walking in the pouring rain and Anselm gets to the camp where his troop leader tells him: "Of course you should have taken the left-handed intrepid carbuncle! It's better than no intrepid carbuncle, isn't it?" They argued, but the troop leader insisted absolutely that Anselm was to march back there in the still-pouring rain and get the left-handed intrepid carbuncle. When he got there, the desk clerk informed him that there was no such thing as an intrepid carbuncle, right-handed or left-handed, and that it was all a joke at his expense, but not to take it too hard because he's not the first and he won't be the last. This made the remaining three miles back to camp still, yes, in the rain, both miserable and humiliating, so when he got back to camp he really lost it on his troop leader, who by then was on the ground laughing, along with everyone else.

But Anselm had a sense of humor about it by the time he was telling me the story, and he had at least half a sense of humor about his dedication to the Boy Scouts as a youth. Yeah, he'd made it to Eagle Scout, and yeah, he was thoroughly into it at the time. But he also turned in his badge a few years ago with that whole Boy Scouts controversy—what was it?—they wouldn't let gay men be adult volunteers for them.

Anselm hated eggs, how could I forget. HATED them. Practically gagged at the mention of them. And he hated babies. He said he didn't like anything that reminded him of birthing or mothers or children, he was still too angry about his own childhood. He told me this when I asked him to come to Jared and Alana's baby shower with me. First he said there was no way he could come, that the whole idea made him feel sick and angry. In the end he decided to come along and it was fine. It was a funny little evening, Jared and Alana in sweatpants (we surprised them), mostly folks from the bookstore there—Stefan, Tim, Andy, me; Tyler had come and gone by the time I got there. And two of Jared's friends from the Midwest, Keith and Curtis. We were all squeezed into the wooden living room, sitting on makeshift seats. It felt really nice to socialize with friends and Anselm. I really wanted that kind of integration, while he always balked at it.

Anselm loved James Joyce, especially *Ulysses*. He loved the modernists. Eliot, Djuna Barnes (especially *Nightwood*), Faulkner.

15 December 2003

I suppose the strong instinct to write the tell-all comes from Catholicism, I thought upon waking today. The concept of a Confessor is so specific, and doesn't get replaced with anything else in society once you leave the Church. I've had the overwhelming urge to confess to my therapist lately—to march in there, get on my metaphorical knees, tell her the worst of what I said to him or thought of him, and have her tell me exactly how I can attain forgiveness. Or is it just that I want her, the listener, to forgive me? The one I dare tell it all to?

Don't get me wrong—I don't want her to help me rationalize anything I've done—I don't want some idiot cheerleader therapist who helps you feel good about yourself no matter what. I want the challenge of someone who cares enough to tell me the absolute truth. And when you're young and involved with the Church, you look for truths there. Stay too long into adulthood and most people start using the Church to keep lying to themselves. But this idea of Confession—I want someone who will help me really look into my heart and clear it of the impurities—to help me back to a state of Grace (that word is almost synonymous with "je ne sais quoi" for me) where my heart is ready to give and receive Love again. *And then she leaves the confession booth and goes back into the world to smile and try and pray and sin again.* In the world outside the Church, "to sin" just means "to experience." To exist in a "state of sin" really just means that you haven't survived your experiences yet. Really, that's all life ever asks of you. Is that you go along, and experience what you experience, and feel what you feel, but that you don't let your experiences bind you up and prevent you from living and seeing and feeling and loving. From moving forward. "Just don't get stuck," that's what Life's saying. "Everything flows," Anselm used to like to quote some Ancient Greek guy. If you don't keep flowing and getting back to the place where your heart can really accept Love and offer it, well, that's the only state of Dis-Grace.

I wonder if anyone besides confessing Catholics or people who've betrayed someone knows what I mean. Well sure, you can hardly make it to age fifteen without hurting someone you love and regretting it terribly. But this feeling--------I can only barely touch it from here. Such an intense longing to love and feel love as you did once as a child, ignorant of what lay ahead, ignorant of the limits and the disappointments and the rejections and the pettiness that dwelt inside even the nicest of people. The longing is to feel such a purity, such an intensity, along *with* the knowledge you've gained in adulthood. But it's hard, so hard one might say it's impossible, though you may have moments or even days or months where you can touch this feeling again. But the rest of the time, it's just the longing for it.

Wasn't this Faust's dilemma? Adam and Eve? The Taint

of Knowledge?

But I digress.

"Vaughn David," that was actually one name, the clan name of the Welsh side of his father's family. But his father went by "Vaughn" as if it was his first name; Anselm never told me what his real first name was, or if he had one. Meanwhile, "Vaughn" looked like Anselm's middle name ("Sellie David" was how he was known growing up), and he didn't take his mother's maiden name until the summer of 2001, from what I could tell. He never told me why he did that. Maybe it had to do with the death of her last brother (the only uncle Anselm knew died in a mine flood) though I think that was some years ago. "Anselm" also comes to him from the Welsh side (even though its origin is clearly German—it suits his face somehow). He said that he was specifically handed down that name because of a ferry pilot or ship's captain that took his family to America, or to France on the way to America. That story would make the most sense if it was the captain of the ship that took them all the way here, but I feel like I remember it being a story about a *ferry*. Anyway, Anselm wasn't the first Anselm in his family. It sounded like it was a namesake that had been handed down for many generations, ever since that ferry ride.

Vaughn David was born in 1938 (a year before my father even though Anselm's four years younger than me) and died in 1977. He died, I mean to say, by his own hand.

Anselm, when I knew him, seemed traumatized by a number of things. Things he could mention but then didn't want to talk about. Things he could generalize about but couldn't mention. Pain that locked him into an anxious body but that wouldn't flow out in tears; he said he's only cried four times in his entire life.

How his father's death affected him he couldn't really say, except that he carried it with him every day of his life. He told me that every morning started with an image of his father's empty bed from that day, washing over his eyes just before he woke. It sounded like that coming-out-of-dream trajectory that I sometimes imagine or even feel as a rising up out of a deep, deep well, or a bottom-less ocean. That feeling of wondering where your body's been all night without you, as you catch the last frame of a dream otherwise lost to the depths. Anselm said that his mind went over every detail, for Anselm discovered his father's absence after his mother had already left the house looking for him. His mind would relive the way the sheets were rumpled and tossed back, the slant of light coming through the window, the smell of summer turning to fall, the scent of his father's sweat in the bed. And he'd wake and have to try and shake off this terrible fear, every morning, like there was still a child's suspense about the scene. "Even since I've been here with you," he told me.

This part is hard to write, I can't profess to know Anselm's private relationship with such a sadness. It was just a fact to know about him; it colored things where you didn't expect it. Like the way Anselm would get terribly upset if anyone referred to him as "masculine" or likened him to Men in the world. He'd grown up without a male role model. Surrounded by women, he chose women as friends; his women friends told him stories of their abuse at the hands of men. He didn't understand men; he didn't trust them; he didn't identify with them. It was a bit of an incongruity because even with his beautiful silky hair that made me mistake women for him all the time, his sturdy Eastern European face was so masculine. And his demeanor as I came to know it, so boyish.

It was a borrowed shotgun. Anselm's father. His job had been at one of the coal mines in the area, and he'd come down with respiratory complications. He may have even been out of work on Disability by then. He was in constant pain, and I guess he suffered from depression as well. It got harder to breathe, and he started to talk less and less. And one morning he showered, shaved, and drove to a motel a few miles away, and by the time Anselm went to wake him up for their usual Saturday morning playtime.... Anselm was four years old.

They told him that his father had died of a heart attack, driving to the store for bacon.

And this was the story Anselm went by for years, until, a few years ago, he had his own heart attack, at age 28. He was on Depakote at the time, a mood stabilizer prescribed to him by an outpatient psychiatrist at Bellevue. Far too high a dose of it, but he didn't know that yet. He was living then with Martin, an asexual uptight Brit who was a thirteenth generation legacy at Oxford, something like that. But they were good as roommates, it sounds like they made fast pals. Martin, I believe, was also in the Music department at Columbia, Ethnomusicology maybe? Or perhaps Music History, if that's separate. I don't remember him being a composer like Anselm, unless I missed that part.

So this particular night—they lived in the apartment in Alphabet City—Anselm happened to be having a one-night stand with a woman from Budapest. And sometime afterwards he realized he was having a heart attack, due to the tingling numbness in his arms and the incredible pain in his chest, and he thought about his dad dying from a heart attack, and he thought he was going to die. He told the Hungarian woman something, and she ran into the living room, naked at 3:00 am, screaming for Martin to *Call an ambulance, Anselm's having a heart attack!*

After the attending doctor told him that the psychiatrist had him on an absurdly high dosage of Depakote, Anselm dropped the pharmaceuticals and the psychiatrists, and never returned to either one since.

I don't remember when it was that Anselm was diagnosed bipolar. Probably sometime after a breakdown at Oberlin, but maybe it was during his year in Vienna.

But we were talking about heart attacks. It was after that experience that Anselm called up his mother and demanded to know—"My father DIDN'T die of a heart attack, did he? I want to know: HOW did my father die?!" So she finally told him.

And some things started to make sense. Like why his mother was obsessed with the question of suicide— Anselm said, it would be a scene something like, an ad or a news item about suicide would appear on the television as they were sitting there watching it together, and suddenly his mother would hit him and start yelling at him: "Don't you ever kill yourself, do you hear me!?!" She told him that all the time, Anselm said.

His mother, truth be told, had endured too many deaths as an adult. The first one was her first fiancé; I believe they were high school sweethearts. He got drafted and sent to Vietnam, then came back with a missing limb and a head full of phantoms. Shot himself in her family's driveway when she still lived at home. (After her husband's suicide, Anselm's grandmother used to wonder out loud what her daughter did to drive her men to self-destruction.) Then there was Anselm's brother, who died, I think, in childbirth. Or was he a stillborn? And there were her own two brothers, both in the mines. And her father's tumor. Anselm guessed that she had just gone into permanent crisis mode. It sounded like she was in a constant state of high anxiety, and then some. Anselm became the scapegoat and the whipping boy for a woman looking for someone to blame: Everything was Anselm's fault, and everything earned him a beating.

Anselm's body learned to deal with it in strange

ways—after a while he could no longer feel nerve-pain, and he'd start laughing in the middle of a beating. "It became the only way I could make her stop," he said. Yeah, Anselm once told me that the only kinds of pain he could feel anymore were migraine, sinus pressure, and what was the third one? Maybe muscle cramps like Charley Horse. I wondered, if he couldn't feel nerve pain, then maybe this had everything to do with why he didn't respond to the caresses I offered him.

"I *am* responding, just not in a way that you want me to," he'd say. Not in a way I can see or experience, I'd think to myself. Not in a way that keeps the back-and-forth going. The lack of it gave me such a profound anxiety. This place of stagnation where one expects life to be so dynamic. Sex is a place of vulnerability; also of regeneration. "One expects," I say, but he'd be so angry. "Who are you comparing me to?! You hold me to impossible expectations!" Our anxieties ricocheted off each other. And my room's so tiny. "Who are you comparing me to?" The question would hang in the air, haunt me. "Everyone I've ever been with, anyone I'd ever want to be with, an alive human being." I never knew what to say, it was overwhelming. Confusing. So painful. Because it was *he* I wanted to be with, it was *he* I wanted to know. For once in my life I was totally present when it mattered, I felt ready to shed my childish fantasies and romantic yearnings. I was ready to call the past the past and be so grateful for what life was giving me now. Grateful *because* of all the disappointments of the other years, the other lovers.

But there's knowing and there's knowing. What I was finding more and more in Anselm were his limitations, and I was losing the Life in him that the Life in me had responded to so wildly. WILDLY! We woke such things up in each other. Twenty page love letters we each wrote. The intensity of our second meeting, when we each fell in love, couldn't understand or admit it until later. One touch of my fingertip on his neck gave him goosebumps all over while we sat in the center of Tompkins Square Park that day, and I could feel the potency on my side, too, could feel my heart in my hands wanting to offer such tenderness as would endear me to him. And there was our first meeting. After our two hour talk at Sophie's, the bar was officially closing (and unofficially staying open for the smoking regulars), and I decided that Cinderella needed to be getting on home. I said goodnight to Anselm and we exchanged numbers, I shook his hand and we also kissed on the cheek goodbye. I walked out, determined to assess the situation when I was sober but not before that. But when I emerged from a nearby deli I'd ducked into to extract cab money from an ATM, Anselm was standing there, on the sidewalk of Avenue B. "Hey stalker," I teased him. He got so shy and stammering. "No—I just—before you left—wanted to say—it was really nice meeting you tonight and—you know, it's *really* hard to meet people in New York...." If I'd had fewer drinks in me, I would have put my hand on his arm and said something reassuring—I was moved by how vulnerable he was letting himself be in front of me, and didn't want to leave him out in the cold. But being so drunk, it was my unchecked instinct to hug him instead. I just meant to hug his thin body for a moment and then step back and say, "It's okay, hon." Not that I gave it so much thought, just that it was that kind of instinct, like to hug a crying teammate or something. I mean, hell, I didn't know anything about this guy.

But what I found was that I wasn't embracing a thin body but a *person* with an open heart. The way Anselm embraced me back, I didn't know what hit me. One minute, I was on Avenue B and 5th Street at 4:00 am, the next minute I was in this place of warmth where there were no shapes, everything just the color brown and the color pink, and the feeling of time stopping, the world stopping. The only thing I was able to understand was that his arms were tightly around me, arms so much stronger than I would have expected from such a sweet, thin young man. I remember thinking, "Who are you?! I'm yours!" It was like I'd never met him before that moment. I couldn't feel my arms, and the rest of me had gone limp inside his grip—I worried that I wasn't transmitting anything at all to him. I kept reminding myself to move my hands across his back, to hold his head and neck, so he'd know I was still there, when in truth, I was lost to this world. But what I didn't realize until later was that my heart was just as open as his—and what we were both feeling was this flooding of heart energy between our bodies. It felt like so long that we stood there like that, before we even thought about kissing. What we were in was already what people pass through kissing to get to.

16 December 2003

Anselm became very ill (with what he didn't say) just after his father died, and he was sick for many months, six months or a year, I forget. His mother was so worried that he wasn't going to make it, but he did, only his ears were never great afterwards. He lost his hearing completely, in fact, in his right ear, and his hearing was only 75% in his left ear. Many years later Anselm was cleaning out his ears with a Q-tip and, I don't know, no one had taught him yet how to use them, so he had the Q-tip too far in his right ear, and when he brought it back out, it had a curious little piece of cartilage on it. So he wrapped it up and took it to the doctor and the doctor looked at it and said, "That's from your deaf ear?" "Yes, sir," Anselm replied. "Yep, that's your ear drum," the doctor told him.

So Anselm was quite completely deaf in his right ear and when we walked anywhere together, I'd have to walk on his left side so we could talk. We slept that way, too, Anselm on the right side of my queen sized futon and me on the left. Which was convenient because then I was right next to the bedroom door and I could let the cat in and out all night when she scratched. Convenient? The cat was such a pain in the ass with the scratching. We'd be all curled around each other, and I'd be cherishing every moment if we were in some really perfect sleeping embrace, because you know, inevitably someone gets cramped or needs to change position for some reason, and the perfect moment is gone. And then the cat would scratch, and I'd try to wait her out, but she'd keep doing it, and I'd picture the door frame getting all shredded up, and the sanding and staining I'll have to do when I move out to pacify the landlord and retain my whole security deposit, and so I'd move just far enough to reach up and turn the door handle and let her out, but even that was far enough to wreck the embrace we were in, so my heart would break a little every time I heard the cat scratch, wondering if my moving away would become his excuse to change positions again.

I have to say, our bodies fit together so, so well. When we spooned it was like being in the womb again, and when we were actually in harmony with each other, laying with our open hearts lined up like that, it was as much love as I could ever want to feel. Anselm had to teach me how to spoon, either I never knew or I forgot. It was the part about the arm under the neck I didn't know—the person who's in back has to ask his lover to lift her head, then he slips his bottom arm under there so he can embrace her with both arms. I loved that feeling of being spooned by Anselm, of sleeping inside such complete embrace. We'd always start out in this position, for all my wondering how he actually felt about us, he'd ask me every single night, "Can I spoon you?" We'd lay there and talk a little, he'd kiss my neck and shoulder and I'd kiss his hand or sometimes turn my face around so we could kiss on the lips goodnight.

But Anselm could never actually fall asleep in that

position, so he'd—after a little while—apologize and say he had to sleep on his stomach or ask if I'd spoon him now. I have to admit, I don't think I held up my end of the bargain with spooning, I only did the arm-under-his-neck thing a few times. The rest of the time I just dealt with the dead arm that lay between us. I'm not sure why, maybe that position just seems wrong to me. Anselm's back is broad enough to make it feel like I was facing a mountain of *back*, it's hard to feel like I could envelope that. It's like when he was in that position, I felt I was being asked to embrace someone who was turning away from me, even though I knew, consciously, that this was not the case.

Nothing felt wrong about it in the mornings. I'd almost always wake up earlier than Anselm did, or at least I'd wake up in a really different state than him. Usually I'd wake up in a state of desire, which I came to think of as the desire of renewal, renewal as morning, a new day being a new chance. For we had many quarrels, many spots of disharmony. But every morning, there we were, doing what I think of as Morning Ballet—the dance of turning our bodies back and forth in half sleep, always in embrace. One time I was dreaming that everywhere our bodies touched each other turned to a blanket of green stamps, like fish scales on our skin. My challenge in the dream was to figure out if the green was the color green of love and growth, or if they were merely food stamps.

Yeah, the sun shines in my window brightly in the mornings, and it's hard to fully sleep through it, even with the dark velvet curtain. So Anselm would wake up, raise his head above my body so he could see the clock, find out the time and yell, "FUCK!" and then usually, "It's too FUCKING EARLY to be awake!" He claimed that he'd picked up this habit from Katy, the pathological liar, his girlfriend from Freshman year of college, who was also his first lover. Sometimes this was really funny to me, one of the things that made him seem like "a real character," and I'd laugh. There were the early days—September and early October—when I'd wake up wanting to sing and dance, no matter what mood he was in. Later, though, it was just a drag.

I just got back from walking over to Bushwick to donate books to a new women's library. It reminded me of the story Anselm told me about the project he and a friend started to get Penguin to donate books to schools in Appalachia. I don't know what exactly they did to get it started, other than propose the possibility and maybe research all the schools in need. Maybe they had to gather specific statistics or even just contact librarians and addresses. In any case, it worked, Penguin Publishing now donates 20,000 books a year (or was that the total thus far?), the Penguin Classics series, to school libraries in Appalachia.

It's Southwestern Pennsylvania that Anselm's from, and he seems to identify with West Virginia just as much as (probably more than) the state of Pennsylvania. He and I each grew up about the same distance from West Virginia, twenty-five minutes' drive, although our towns are worlds apart. Greene County, Pennsylvania being in the mountains and in the very poorest area of America. And Loudoun County, Virginia being at the foothills and in the wealthy Horse Country suburbs of Washington. The school Anselm went to (I don't know if it was a few towns away or what) was everything in one—grade school, middle school, high school—he went there Kindergarten through Twelfth Grade. His graduating class was something really small, under 30 people. Anselm didn't have any friends growing up, although he once told me he has no idea what the words "lonely" or "bored" mean. "I hear other people say those words, but I've never experienced anything I'd call by those names," he said.

Anselm's county is home of the longest-running fair in America, the Jacktown Fair; but the King Coal Parade is almost as big a deal, and the two have kind of divided along the lines of Celtic heritage versus Slavic immigrants. Anselm's grandmother on his father's side was once crowned Queen of the Jacktown Fair, whereas his aunt with Croatian/Ukrainian blood was runner-up for Coal Queen the year she graduated high school. Anselm said the area is very dense with black coal in particular, which is softer and more hazardous to the lungs than other kinds of coal. That means it's more dangerous both to coal miners and to anyone downwind of the burning. Anselm also said that so many soldiers were drafted from his county to the front lines of the Vietnam War that whole towns lost a generation of men.

Anselm's county was one of the last in America to still have corporal punishment in the school system. Though it's long been banned by federal law, they got around it by making it a consensual, optional punishment. I guess the alternative was something people wanted even less—long detentions, expulsion, or something that'd go down on the dreaded Permanent Record. So the vast majority "took their licks" if or when that question came up. The paddle on the behind. Anselm talked about having to take it from his favorite teacher, the music teacher who was the closest thing Anselm had to a father figure, the person who made sure that Anselm got out of Appalachia. I can't remember if it actually involved Anselm having to drop his drawers or not. He was being punished for something involving Student Council, a teacher trying to veto a student vote, and Anselm strongly (philosophically) objecting, stating "Fuck THAT" and walking out of the room. And there was the part about Anselm having to sign a release form that he was willingly submitting to the paddle, that was ultimately how they got around the legalities. Then the form was on your record until you graduated, but no longer than that.

I expressed some shock and sympathy that this still went on during his time there, but Anselm protested. He said that since they've finally abolished it there, he's watched the students walk all over the rules, have no respect for their elders; the fights, he said, are out of control. Students can be violent to an alarming degree and the teachers can't even pull them off each other, lest they get sued. He said he thought it was a system that definitely worked to keep order among the ranks.

It was the incident with his sister that made him realize that he had to get as far from this place as soon as he could. That he was *from* this place, but he would no longer be *of* them.

One afternoon, Anselm was in his room tinkering with his chemistry set, and his sister and her best friend were out in the backyard. Then he heard them come into the house; as Anselm tells it, the two girls barged into his room and pushed him flat onto his bed before he knew what was happening. The friend sat on him (she was the healthy, big-boned type) and held his arms down while Leeanne looked him directly in the eye and started taking off her clothes. At first, Anselm was startled enough to stay pinned down, under the weight of horror and surprise. But soon he regained his strength and his voice: "GET OUT!" he shouted as he tore himself out of the friend's grip. Anselm was then fifteen and his sister, thirteen.

Who am I to say? But it seemed that a deep wound of Betrayal set inside Anselm at that moment, and of course the anger that went with it. And mistrust and hardness became the shell that kept her from hurting him ever again—he said he never looked her in the eye again, it sounded like he barely ever spoke to her afterwards. Just locked his bedroom door and that was that. Before she graduated high school, Leeanne ended up running out of town with an elementary school teacher, but married a different fellow and now lives in Cedar Rapids (he thinks). He doesn't even know her married name. Says it will probably take their mother dying for them to ever have a relationship. The one thing that they have in common, he told me, is that fact that they both ran far away from their mother.

I told Anselm once that I hadn't stopped thinking about him since we met. And it looks like that's still true.

17 December 2003

Anselm never cared about the finishing of a piece of music, about the finished product, he only cared about the writing of the piece while he was in it. He made it sound like finished products were children he'd already forgotten about—what he loved was the act of the writing. The transcribing of the sounds in his head and heart. "What is music as opposed to poetry?" I said. "All the shades of emotions that have no words—that are in between," he said. He made it sound like he conceived of a vast and dense cosmos of subtle emotions, even if he could only express most of them in musical terms.

If I think about it, I do and I don't associate Anselm with music. I don't associate music with "us," for instance. We didn't have an "our song," and I'm not even sure we had any musical tastes in common. I remember Anselm DJ-ing for us on my boom box, but right now the only things I can remember him playing were the Elliott Carter album (one of his favorites) or the mix-CD that Jen made him after he told her he just wanted to be friends. I can't remember any of the specific songs, though—it was all 90s rock and pop, which just washes over my ears like it's not there—those jaded voices just never stick with me.

I remember Anselm inviting me to write a libretto for an opera he would compose—this was when we were still on the phone. I remember sitting at Irina's desk in the basement, staring at the chunky, square touch-tone as we talked after my bookstore shift. We were going to enter a contest he knew about; the prize was tens of thousands of dollars and a production in Paris. I was both flattered and daunted, but anyway the conversation was probably more about comprehending our relationship at that moment and trying on mutual fantasies of a future together. I was excited, too; the idea made me think of a story I read about Edna St. Vincent Millay writing an opera, the twenty minutes of standing ovations she received at the Met, and how it helped her become one of the most famous living poets of her time, and surely one of the best compensated. For that opera she earned the kind of money poets don't even dream about, unless they play Lotto.

But music was surely part of Anselm's language, and most of how he understood the world. His drive to write music seemed to be about putting the world together in patterns that made sense and beauty. It seemed double-edged—one part was an ordering inside himself, like sometimes when he was thinking out loud, his fingers started playing piano keys that weren't there. Another part was always an offering, a way out of his own skin and into the world, a bridge between himself and the universe. Anselm described it even more poetically in one of his letters. He talked about an ancient music theory from South America or maybe India. It says that music inhabits the world, the air around us, and all musicians have to do is find their way to that realm. All the music that ever was or will be already exists and it's just waiting for us to be patient and sensitive enough hear it. He wrote me a word in that foreign language that translates to "ocean of sound" or "ocean of music."

Another time he wrote me about the Sicilian *tarantella*. That's the medieval folkdance where a bitten one dances frenetically enough to get a spider's poison out of the body. He wrote that in a letter when he finally told me that he was falling in love with me—that was the "poison" he said he was writing frantically around and could no longer hold inside himself. Even then, he had to call me and say it to me on the phone right after he mailed the letter; he was terrified that he was telling me in a way that he wouldn't see my reaction. He told me when I was sitting in the phone booth at Bea's, with the door half open because it was so humid. I thought he was about to tell me something awful; he sounded sick to his stomach as he was trying to get the words out. When he finally delivered what he had to say, I was so relieved.

[Later]

"I love you *so* much, " he whispered to me in the dark, embracing me as we lay there. He had just made love to me. It was the night he'd come home to find me suffering from a migraine. "I love you *so* much," he said it exactly as directly and tenderly as I wanted to hear him speak to me. "Do you *feel* loved by me?" He was speaking in his real voice that night. "Do you *feel* loved by me?" He said it with enough pathos to break my heart a little. Made me feel his yearning to know if his love *worked*, did what he want me to know *reach* me? It was I who spoke in the false voice that night. I replied with some kind of strained "Yes," for we'd fought the night before, and I'd doubted everything. "Do you feel loved by me?" Also in the plaintive whisper. The answer now is a true *Yes*, if only for this one memory.

I just wanted the *chance* to love him--------we were always passing by each other. I reached out, but he couldn't believe in my love. It's this faithlessness in me that stabs the sharpest. To feel so impotent in loving someone! I offered—he was so skeptical. My offerings—some he took for granted, some he called disingenuous, some he couldn't respond to in kind, some he couldn't see at all.

We both tried—he tried in his ways that were cryptic to me as well. We passed by each other, speaking cryptic languages the other hadn't learned.

Our second day together, after his return—a strange day, spent at Coney Island, he didn't want to be intimate with me, didn't really want to talk. It sat so wrong with me—I knew even then he wasn't the lover I'd thought he was. I don't mean it superficially—I mean I knew there was a missing connection with sex, physical affection in him. (This after six weeks of our outrageous romancing through the phone lines, through the U.S. mail.) I felt drained; I felt sick. I had a terrible stomachache by lunchtime, eating on the boardwalk at Brighton. Then walking back to the train—we walked down side streets all the way to Avenue X, the trains weren't running through to the Coney stop—

I almost fainted several times.

Back home I felt better and he felt worse, mood-wise. He wanted us to go out to some bars in Williamsburg. Getting ready in the mirror and feeling the acute lack of the day's affection, I snapped. "I'm *so* ugly," I blurted, and stormed off to the safety of the dark kitchen.

He was genuinely concerned. We talked in the dark kitchen; we talked in the dark living room; he coaxed me back into the lighted bedroom. I was having a panic attack the whole time, or maybe it was just the hysteria of not having the courage to say: "*What* are you trying to *do* to me?"

By the time we got into the bedroom, I had a full-blown meltdown, internalizing his daylong inattentiveness into an inescapable feeling of ugliness and impotence, and just general ineffable anguish. I remember especially the feeling of him holding me on the bed to try and comfort me, holding me with all his might, and it comforted me not at all.

Unbearable. To think of how we passed by each other. Or to think of the two Anselms. In this memory, as in the memory of the migraine, there was the Anselm who was comforting me, loving me so very sweetly, when I was in so much pain that the other Anselm had caused me.

18 December 2003

Anselm hated any foods that were "too healthy," and when he felt himself getting a cold he believed in the "blood alcohol cure." Which is, he'd drink a heavy evening's worth of hard liquor so it would kill the germs in his blood, he said that worked for him. He used to say no one could call themselves an American before they'd had the Patriotic Triptych: Bourbon, Rye, and Moonshine.

There's times when Anselm really hates the subways. His body surrounded by the chrome of the subway car. When he's slipping into the bad space, a subway car is one of the worst places he can be. He says it's like an echo chamber for the psyche. Everything bad he's thinking and feeling becomes more and more abstract and doubles back on him.

He really hates transfer tunnels. Like the one at Seventh Avenue and 14th Street, between the IRT and the F line. He can barely articulate why he hates them so much, he'll just tell you with vehemence that he'd rather go outside and pay again than use those block-long underground tunnels. With their stagnant air, crush of passengers, no pretense of windows, lit only by fluorescent light, which he loathes.

I remember getting out of the train at that stop, 14th Street and Seventh Avenue, where would we have been coming from? Was it the time we went to the brunch party at Serena's place? That was a disaster. Anselm was in a terrible mood, whatever the occasion was. He wanted to get out of the underground level as fast as possible. We were on the wrong end of the subway, having just barely caught the train in Brooklyn; when we got out, we were a bit disoriented in the station. We went up some stairs that let out at 12th or 13th Street. But when we turned the corner after the first landing, there were black metal gates blocking the rest of the way. "Why don't they TELL you?" Anselm was angry and panicked. We walked back along the platform to find the 14th Street exit instead.

People tell me sometimes, "Oh, yeah, New York City is really bad for anyone who is mentally ill." I don't often think of Anselm as mentally ill. Just as someone who has crazy Midwestern ideas of sex and relationships and is angry most of the time.

Anselm basically hated New York by the end. I mean, I guess he felt defeated by it. He never found a job again, although I had no evidence that he was looking, either. I asked him if there was a place we could go and be together, to Chicago or Marseilles or some other city we could try, but he just ignored me and kept bemoaning New York. I suppose I hoped our love still existed perfectly-intact somewhere in the ether, or maybe I didn't think that at all but I wanted to see what he'd say. After that conversation I had to go to work, and he stayed there on the bench in McCarren Park and watched me go, and watched me stop and admire the baseball field full of pigeons as I came upon it. Yeah, he told me later that he looked at me standing there for a while, and it surprised me that he still took an interest in what I was about. I had no sense of it anymore.

19 December 2003

Anselm's fears were hard to predict. They came on sudden and strong, like the morning of September 11th when he was sitting having a leisurely coffee in Café Dante and heard about the Tower falling, and he left for the nearest subway so quickly he forgot to pay his bill. When he got to Williamsburg, he went into a bodega to get a coke, and the guy behind the counter was watching it on television. But Anselm didn't understand what was going on—his mind had already blocked the event out, somewhere during the trip under the East River.

At times, Anselm could walk away from fears like I wouldn't expect, unless walking away was just what he did with them. One morning in November, we woke up to endless fire trucks screaming past Kingsland, it sounded like it was coming from the BQE. It's the kind of thing you try to sleep through on your day off, hoping it's just one or two vehicles and it won't reach your conscious brain. But the sirens just kept coming. Eventually my brain reminded me that these were endless sirens *in a post 9/11 world,* and Anselm and I sat up all at once like we'd had the same thought at the same moment. For a minute, I thought it was something that could bring us close together again. I actually thought it might be a bad day in the world but a good day between us.

When I was really young, I wove deeply romantic fantasies around situations like this—emergencies where two scared and lonely people fell into fervent embraces to comfort each other, in part because all normal social decorum was out the window. The scenarios always involved a deep seriousness: me and my fantasy beau joining forces to face unthinkable tragedies and insurmountable odds, and the seriousness itself was romantic. But not me and Anselm. I had barely turned my back to hover over the radio and gather the bad news from 1010 WINS when he was dressed and halfway out the door. "Wait—!" I pleaded after him, and it felt like so many moments between us: I was always wondering where he was disappearing to now, and why I wasn't invited.

Just this minute, I have no memory of where he said he was going. Was he off to write music in some café on Bedford, was he meeting Jen uptown at Fairway, had Ethan and Andrea come back to New York from Glasgow already? Sometime after he left, I headed to the luncheonette when the headlines failed to produce any mention of Brooklyn bombings.

As it turned out, it was a five-alarm fire. A whole block was up in flames, on the side of the park near the good pizza place, and Bea was there at the luncheonette collecting tidbits of information, passing them along, and shaking her head, her brow furrowed. "Tsk, tsk, tsk." Bea's was like a community center for non-Polish Greenpoint, so many families had been going there a long time. She's been open at least two generations worth by now. When she laments (in her oblique way) that my upstairs neighbor, Jeannie, has a drug problem and lost custody of the baby, it's likely that she's known Jeannie since she was a baby herself. While I was sitting at the counter, Francis told me he knew one family on that block who'd owned their building since at least the 1930s. Then Richard came in and told us that the Grabowski's roof had just collapsed, but everyone had gotten out alright, including the dog. (When I say Bea's is the center of non-Polish Greenpoint, that includes Polish-Americans too, for whatever reason—-I guess because they're really just long-time Brooklynites and don't mix in the same networks with the newly-immigrated Polish.) The old fellow who writes poems (Henry?) came by and said it looked like nine houses were still burning and no sign of the flames letting up. Later I found out a younger poet had been affected by the fire, had lost his apartment and a few years worth of writings. Victor was the one who told me—I think it was one of the poets he published in the early days, back when his press was still xerox copies.

It's funny, as much as I associate Bea's phone booth with Anselm, I don't remember going to the luncheonette with him more than a few times once he got back to New York, and I don't remember him caring about it much when we went. It's another thing that seems to make him slither out of my hands in memories. This place that was the center of so much love, so much good will, so much communication, decades of connections—-and Bea, who was like my grandmother and my Oracle of Delphi-—I brought more than one boyfriend to her to receive her blessing. How was it possible to bring Anselm into the middle of this place and still have all these things evade us?

Within a few days of the fire, Bea had a sign up that said they were collecting money to help the families.

[Later]

There was the night Anselm and I were up late and giddy (moments like these felt all-forgiving); we were trying to get to sleep but there was no more Tylenol PM. Finally I found some Advil in my bag, the kind that comes in gel capsules, which relaxed us even further—I think it hits the bloodstream really fast. We felt drunk; everything suddenly got hilarious. We were lying side by side, not spooned, on the futon and both staring at the ceiling or the wall (my room's so small and undecorated), and it was late in the time he was here. And it occurred to me to say, "It's like we're on a really weird road trip together...." It doesn't even make that much sense now but it seemed dead-on at the time, for better or for worse. We laughed and laughed.

It's true that we were almost always alone. There was the time Francesca invited us to a party at her new place, a shared apartment in this warehouse out in Bushwick, the one where Raymond says he used to go to write on the loading dock when he was basically homeless. The building was still part active sweatshop, with the Central American seamstresses clocking in and out from their shifts in the front hallway, I think it was underwear. In the waning evening light, Anselm and I walked along Morgan

Avenue from Greenpoint the whole way there (and back, too, which was probably unwise).

I no longer remember the order of everything—was this before the fire and after the night Anselm didn't get home until 7:00 a.m., creeping in with some story about horribly delayed L service and making his way across the Williamsburg Bridge, uphill both ways in the rain? It was definitely before Francesca discovered she had bed bugs and started sleeping under mosquito netting. Anyway, I do remember that I wanted Francesca to meet Anselm—I still embraced those things that might bring our desert-island existence into some three-dimensional reality. I still sought social realms that might solidify us into being a real relationship, one where you enjoy being together as two among the masses, and then suddenly two alone again with newfound topics of conversation.

But of course Anselm was so skittish among the living. He was already starting to waver as we approached the bodega near Francesca's building, where he got a few Slim Jims and a six pack of Old Milwaukee (he only drinks Guinness when *others* are buying), and I got a Mexican soda, a bag of plantain chips, and a two liter of Diet Coke. As we walked up the concrete stairs (I think she was on the 3rd floor), Anselm decided he wanted to drink at least some of his beer on the roof before we went in. And then (I could not have predicted this), we never went in. We sat for over two hours on the roof next to the translucent sky-light that communicated to the main room of the party, me pointing out Francesca's voice, and then Tyler's; Anselm telling stories ("This reminds me…"); Anselm finishing his beer and then most of the Diet Coke; us laughing at "our" ridiculous trepidation. Frankly, I kept thinking we'd go in eventually. But I was torn. We were having an unlikely good time with each other—there was an ease between us that I hated to test by relocating. We were dressed warmly enough for the November weather, which anyway wasn't terribly punishing. But of course I also had the foreboding sense that Anselm and I were always going to be only an intangible, fleeting entity, if we never dared to enter real life together. To Anselm, the party was anything but "real life"—it was people being fake, it was horseshit. But for me, real life was wherever the most people were gathered, and even more so if my friends were involved.

20 December 2003

Anselm never gave money to anyone who begged for it on the street. Not that he was hard-hearted, only that he didn't believe in begging. I think he thought the people who actually asked for it didn't need it as much as some others. Once when his mother wired him the most money she ever wired him when he lived with me ($100), he put $50 in the cup of a fellow sleeping on 14th Street. Another time—our last time at Sophie's, a few days before he left town—we were on our way back inside the bar from a smoke break. It was cold and raining out—we'd been under an awning. We passed a skinny black woman who was rummaging through the outdoor ashtray, looking for butts that were long enough to smoke. Anselm tapped her on the back and gave her one of his good ones, a Nat Sherman. She was so poor, you couldn't tell until she spoke whether she was a man or a woman. "Is that your wife?" she asked him about me. Anselm was talking to someone and didn't answer. "Is that your wife?" she asked again. She had a huge smile on her face as she looked at him. The second time I answered quickly, "Yes." She turned to me for a moment before looking back at him admiringly, "Your husband sure is GOOD looking!"

Inside the bar I laughed at myself—"Did you hear how quickly I called myself your wife?" "Yes I did," he said. "I'm flattered."

—Now I've just checked my voice mail on the corner payphone, and Anselm's left me a message; I didn't expect it at all. I cried to hear his voice. All kindness and full-throated yin as he is when he calls from Pennsylvania. I don't know whether it's the rural setting or the loneliness (surely he must experience something like The Yearning For Company when he's there, he doesn't see anyone but his mother) or simply the distance from the person he's calling, but he sounds so much different when he's calling from there.

When he got off the bus on September 11th, when he came back to me, I was surprised to see such a masculine face.

I'm remembering his hands, which looked like a cross between those of a farmer and a piano player. Tapered but work-worn. Thin, intelligent, long fingers but a sure, passionate grip. And the scar on the first knuckle of his right hand.

He did do farm work for money, growing up. Said that was about the only work there was left. His county claims something like 12% unemployment, but that's just the folks collecting the checks. It's more like 85% of the people that are unemployed. There's simply no jobs there, he said. And yet it doesn't stop anyone from buying huge trucks that put them into debt and riding around getting into trouble. Too much time on their hands to be up to anything but no-good. He said prostitution, perversion, drug use are quite high.

When his friend Jen went to visit him from Akron before she went back to Columbia for the fall, she couldn't believe the place. She said it was so much worse than she'd imagined. Anselm said so many of the folks there look like the "Deliverance" cliché—distorted Down-syndrome faces. And then there's the weekly Sunday KKK meetings ("rallies"?) in his town. And the nearby car repair shop, Kuhntown Kar Kare.

But then some of Anselm's favorite places are there, too. Like Ten Mile Creek, the Monongahela River, and of course the spot where two rivers converge down near McKeesport. When he was home in August, he said after a rainstorm (with high winds) that he forgot the force Nature could become there—bending gargantuan trees like it was nothing to Her.

Funny that he should call tonight—he said he was calling to see how I was, to say hi, and to wish me a safe trip if I was traveling for the holidays. The buzz was all over the news today about whether they were going to raise the terrorist alert from code yellow to code orange over the holidays, or not. They've gotten threats but only vague ones. As soon as I heard his message, it made me think—Anselm would still, I believe, be the first person I'd try to call. Would he still care?

[Later]

War and abuse are on the same scale in my mind—both hard to move on from because hard to mourn. The combination of emotions, experiences—it produces as much anger as pain. The necessary line of offense-as-defense. Anger is a mask, numbness and depression another level of masking. Daily routine of pointless work tasks is one form of numbness.

What is war? A sustained aggression where there doesn't need to be one. Higher-ups orchestrating these forums for absolute aggression, carried out by and inflicted upon people who have no choice in the matter. Thousands living in fear and emergency adrenaline levels. Exhaustion.

What is abuse? Someone with an upper hand taking advantage of it over a more vulnerable someone, usually exactly where there should have been intimacy, trust, love instead.

I'm finding it very hard to mourn Anselm. I haven't been able to cry much yet. Writing this, there's such a confusing mix of emotions that I get so bound up. It seems like a full-time task to try and trace which emotions are which. And what my relationship to them is. Since Anselm left I've been eating constantly, as if to stuff the emotions down into the body, below the level of my consciousness.

21 December 2003

Solstice.

There was the blackout, that Thursday in August when Anselm was still in Pennsylvania. I left my house to go to the luncheonette and noticed just as I was leaving that my lights didn't work. I thought it was our building, then Charlie from downstairs told me it was the whole neighborhood. Ruth said there was a crowd of men outside the OTB on Meserole waiting for the screens to come back on. Bea thought she heard it was in Queens, too, and maybe Manhattan, but when a fellow came by her window and said that Boston and Philadelphia were dark, a bolt of fear went through me, and then the word "terrorism" went around the place and I got on the phone to Anselm right away. No, but he wasn't home (for once—he was always home!) so I had him call me back on the luncheonette payphone, that was the usual thing, because I haven't had a home phone since I got evicted in March. The phone at the diner is still 50 cents for unlimited time, and it still takes calls from outside, and there's a wooden booth you can sit in and close the door, so it's good. I called Anselm from there all of August unless I called him from work.

While I was waiting for him to call me back, all I could think of was how unbearable it would be to be separated by terrorism, or if it would prevent him from coming back to the city, etc. And I knew that my heart was really with this guy, though I'd known him a little less than two weeks then. It wasn't too long before he called back. He was watching CNN, so he knew more than I did about it all. It seemed that most of the North East (but not, actually, Boston) had lost their power due to a kind of Domino effect after the power went down in one place—we were all discovering that the nation (or the North East, at least) operates on a Grid System. America was blaming it on Canada, and Canada said it started in America. Eventually everyone blamed it on Ohio.

Anselm just wished he was in New York. He imagined all the revelry that was going to go on, the all night street parties and the music and the dancing. He wished he could be at his pub, Sophie's. He asked me what I was planning to do that night, and I just felt like an old lady for planning to go home before dark, barricade myself against terrorism and looting.

He was right, in fact, about the parties, and I was wrong about the looting. (Being that Anselm's only been in New York on and off since '98, he's often better at describing the climate of *new* New York than I am—I still see New York for what it *was*.) In Williamsburg, an impromptu marching band walked the streets all night, and in Tompkins Square, friendly bonfires raged. Only two incidents of looting were reported in the whole city—one in Bed Stuy, and one in SoHo.

I can't believe Anselm is back with his mother, of all places. They seem like star-crossed lovers to me, I mean born under a bad star. After the loss of one fiancé and one husband, she needed someone as a partner and a place to deposit a whole lot of feelings. Anselm, I think, became both of those things. I know she wasn't sexual with him, but she took the aggressive part of the sexual instinct and made Anselm her sparring partner instead of her lover. There was a not-really-told story about her sadistically tickling him. I don't know if this was when he was young but I can imagine so, as if her instinct to beat him started with tickling instead. Consequently, any caresses I gave Anselm, if he felt them at all, were experienced as tickling and as sadistic, and he would push my hands off him or tell me to stop. The same with certain kisses. It got to be that I conceived of the shaft of his penis being the only place that I was allowed to touch him that had feeling. (There were places I was forbidden to go.) And I couldn't help it, I thought, "That kind of bodymap seems like the definition of fascism."

Later his mother, crazy Leo that she was, seemed to goad him into entering the fights. For Anselm told me about one incident of hitting her back to get her off of him; I can't remember if he implied there were others. It just makes the most sense to me, for it doesn't seem that she would hit him just when she was mad, but that she would find excuses to be mad at him so she could enter the sparring match. Anselm, too, seemed to invent reasons to be mad at me, or even at himself, so that we could fight when nothing was actually wrong, as much love as we had; as much as I (once, we) really wanted to come to understanding. It was like he would find things to be alienated over. When we were already connected at the heart, and there was no reason! And there were all the fights I heard about between him and Catherine, his "ex-fiancée"—usually drunken bar scenes. Sophie's, in fact, was the only date Anselm ever actually took me on, and I resisted at least half of the invitations. Because it would always turn into drama. Either a seemingly-invented fight or problem, or even a series of romantic declarations that seemed too dramatic and out of the blue to be indicative of true feelings. For true feelings are what come out of intimacy, in alone moments, so if he couldn't declare things to me there, why would I accept his professions at the pub?

Slowly I got wise to this and had no interest in meeting him at the bars after a while. Even all the stories he'd tell about the other regulars just sounded like a gaggle of drama queens performing for each other. But Anselm learned to bring the bar home: though I told Anselm I hated mixing men and alcohol, it wasn't since mid-October that we'd had sober sex. Or should I say *he*.

I did forgive Anselm for this somewhat when I started to realize that he couldn't even begin to accept his body when he was sober. Another reason that I think his mother invited him into the fights: the depth of shame that lived in his body and self image. It was more than just from the horror of being done to; it seemed like the horror of what he'd done. What someone had goaded him to do. Catherine, too—the emotional sadist and sexual masochist. She'd insist that they were having sex *now*, even if he was depressed, or she'd goad him into a huge fight so that he'd dominate her, and do other things, I don't know. Go from not being in the mood, to sexing her as sadistically as she wanted. It got so he was cutting himself—his arms—a few months before he was hospitalized that summer.

Anselm once said, "The ONE night of true intimacy in TWO YEARS with Catherine was the night we got stranded on the side of the road in a blizzard, on the way back from Montréal. The heat in the rental car was broken, and we had to hold each other all night for fear of freezing to death." He told me this when he and I were embraced similarly, the one or two cold nights in October before the landlord turned the heat on. It was one of his many stories that began, "This reminds me of the time...." Sometimes I felt like his emotional stenographer, like he was looking back over his whole life and dictating it to me. I would wonder about his attraction to writers. Did he want to hand his life story to someone else who might make sense of it?

22 December 2003

Anselm's favorite insult was "disingenuous." His fa-vorite "pop" was Diet Mountain Dew. He was hypo-glycemic, which meant that he was always slightly dehy-drated, AND that he couldn't have too much sugar (except sometimes when he needed pure sugar, right away), so he sucked down diet soda all day long. Mostly, like I said, Diet Mountain Dew, but sometimes Diet Pepsi or Diet Coke with Lemon. He always had to pee. Every half hour, I'd say. He *did* consume a *lot* of liquid, soda and coffee and beer and sometimes whiskey, but he said he never had to pee so much before he had kidney problems in Europe. Now I can't remember if this story is from the time he went to Austria before he went to France for the second time. There were stories from Vienna about drinking coffee all day and Tokay all night with his "colleagues." There was the time—from our phone days in August—that I told him that I didn't really drink coffee, and he said, "Oh, and I really want to take you to Austria with me, but are you going to be like April? I took April to Austria the second time I went, and she didn't drink coffee or alcohol, so she'd just SIT THERE while I caroused with my colleagues...." But I think the kidney story was from France. He was in Paris and he started peeing blood, so he went to the hospi-tal. The doctor asked Anselm how much coffee he'd had to drink that day and he said 18 cups. So the doctor put him off coffee for awhile, and he's been peeing every half hour ever since.

Anselm was a Cancer with a Pisces moon—so much water, I thought when I first found this out. Now it just makes me picture him like one of his rivers—his mood endlessly shifting in subtle gradations. One has to sit very still and pay close attention to see where he's going, where he's gone. Blink and he's fallen into a whole new persona.

Ironic because in other ways he was so stubborn, almost stagnant. We fought about this, my belief that everything is dynamic, that every ill is repairable. In the beginning, when he was in Pennsylvania reading my novel, it was him telling me, "I love the way you're so aware of your own BECOMING. You're always fluid, in motion." Later I found out, "It's a quality I'm capable of admiring in someone else, not because I cultivate it in myself." Still later I heard, "I can be working towards something, everything in my life can be going along great, and then BOOM." Depression comes along and wipes the slate clean again.

23 December 2003

Tonight I heard the awful noises coming from upstairs again—Jeannie and one of her guys fighting. First it's the yelling back and forth, and then the pounding starts— I can never tell whether that's a beating happening or very vigorous sex. Luckily Jeannie spends most of her time these days at the front of the building. When her mom was alive, they talked at the kitchen table a lot, right above my head, but that was in softer tones, almost comforting.

Anselm and I didn't fight very often, not outright. But when we did, it always seemed like the stakes were every-thing, winner take all, and if someone said the wrong word, we were willing to burn the whole thing to the ground.

I'd always imagined fighting with a lover as a much more playful give-and-take, a loud honesty, an exaggerated airing-out. It must be from watching too many mid-centu-ry movies: "Just you wait, 'Enry 'Iggins," "You forget I'M in AmER-ica!" or "Maggie the Cat is ALIVE!" Willful women who were still adored by their men at the end of the script.

Burn the whole thing to the ground. Fighting with Anselm terrified me. What "thing" did I think there was to burn? The stakes were sky-high in my mind, or do I mean my fears? I remember this sharp contrast from the weeks we spent apart. Our letters, our hopes, discovering all we shared—we built something so beautiful that neither of us could fully believe that it was here to stay. I remember floating around the bookstore, walking around my life feeling *high*. I couldn't eat, couldn't sleep—this energy—LOVE—coursing through me, keeping me restless. But every ten days or so, I would crash completely. My mood, my body—I'd sleep for hours. Anselm wouldn't recognize my voice on the phone and his anxieties would flare up, start fueling mine. I begged him to come back to New York so we could see what was real. The longer he stayed away, the taller our dreams soared, and the more dangerous we became to ourselves.

24 December 2003

On a train to D.C.

Massages are one of the things Anselm calls "disingenuous." Massage never had any effect on him, he said, though he'd had them at the hands of both friends and professionals. So he found it to be an activity that seemed manipulative on the part of the person wanting to give him a massage (wanting to induce a certain effect); then soon frustrating for both parties.

When I picture him and massage, it's on an old wooden porch in Ohio—Oberlin or Granville. A female friend of his was giving him a massage after she returned from her shift at the exotic dancing joint. She was doing this one summer while she saved up to go to Turkey for a year or a semester. I'm not sure if he described her as "friend" because it was in the beginning and he was still sparing my feelings, or if this was Meredith, or if it was some other "friend" like Meredith. I guess Meredith might have been described as a "friend" since they were both in relationships with other people at the time.

In any case his friend gave him a massage while she deconstructed her day at the exotic dancing lounge. Deconstructed as in sliced it up in terms of Marxist, feminist, post-colonial, post-visual, Lacanian, Hegelian, cultural critical theory. I think Anselm was telling me as an example of her as an unlikely stripper, as a stripper who was also a complex feminist and a strong woman, but much later he told me another story that she got as messed up over the experience as anyone else he'd ever heard of. Though she did make it to Istanbul.

He told me there was far too much anxiety in his body for massage to work on him, as in, the years he'd spent living with anxiety in his muscles. When he told me this, I still thought it was mostly an effect of the depression itself, the fear of being in the bad space and not knowing how long it would last. And it was, partly.

25 December 2003

The last time that Anselm and I kissed as long and as passionately as I always imagined kissing him was the first night we met. For two hours after Sophie's closed we sat at a bus stop on First Avenue and 23rd Street, we couldn't get enough of each other. There was passion, hunger, tenderness. And our second meeting was beautiful, but it was more about touch than about kissing. Every caress was magnified, Anselm later said, by the taste of longing, by our impending separation. The kissing that day was very intimate, spare, deliberate more so than hungry and endless.

When Anselm returned to New York, there was only kissing that went along with sex, or sterile kind of marriage-pecks. The latter being the kind of kisses that seemed to keep my desire at bay rather than open me up. I was terribly confused. And then the biting slowly started to take over. Anselm's passionate kissing during sex turned into hard biting—of my lips, my tongue, my chin—so hard that at least once every time the words would flash through my mind, "This guy hates women." He'd bite my breasts, too. Though I tried to tell him that was crossing a line for me, it seemed *too* misogynous.

Today whenever I'd think of Anselm, it all seemed like it had happened an extremely long time ago. Feeling of coldness and distance.

26 December 2003

He said that with Catherine, if he did get in the mood on his own, he would be very dominant with her, before she could assert her own will. This story was evident in many moments in our love-making. He was quick and forceful and dominating but in a way that seemed to have to do with his relationship to Woman much more so than to me. Like there were energies he was trying to ward off. He wanted to please a woman in order to conquer her, not in order to open her up, expand her desires. He sometimes made me think of a line from Fleetwood Mac, "Rulers make bad lovers, better put your kingdom up for sale------." Anselm wasn't a bad lover, not at all. He knew exactly what he was doing; he knew a woman's body to an eerie degree. But that, too, could be a power play when he wanted to use it that way. Later I'd imagine him as if he was trying to tame the Wicked Witch—his mother, his sister, Catherine. His dominant side seemed so filled with anxiety, so haunted.

I wanted so much for him to be present—with his own body, with mine. I'm realizing that there was a part of him that he never let me close to—his true sadness, his youngest self, as Francesca and I used to say, his "Little Me." He could tell me stories, he could act out certain vulnerabilities, but I don't know that he was ever able to be present with his wounded self, the one I hoped my love, our love, could heal.

"Everything flows," Anselm would say to this. He felt I was so critical of him and expected things to change too quickly. I feared, in the darkest moments, that I wasn't any different from his sadist girlfriends: We had the same frustration with his lack of desire, just that I took out my frustration in huffing and puffing episodes and belabored talks and letters—instead of insisting on the sex Anselm didn't want to have. At least I'm not a rapist. But Anselm still told me, "It's a power play. If you get angry with me because I don't want to have sex, that's a power play."

It's true, I didn't have the kind of patience he was asking of me. Not inherently, but contextually: The relationship he offered me didn't inspire the kind of patience he asked of me.

27 December 2003

What do I really know about Anselm? Only what he told me. I never met anyone who could give me a context for him, flesh out his existence. There were no co-workers to meet, we never ran into his friends, his mother never answered the phone. There was no place I could go and see Anselm living his life without me, like a job or a school or even an apartment. This was it. My four walls and our two faces and the stories he was constantly telling me. Was he a truthful whitefoot or a lying blackfoot? After I invited him into my house, it seemed better to believe him than to wonder.

Well, of course there was Sophie's. How could I forget. I met his drinking chums—the guys who happened to be fixtures at a bar he frequented. It's about as useful as saying I met six of his favorite barstools.

I guess there were moments when I doubted, or maybe it was a hum that was starting to sound underneath everything. Once when Anselm made us watch "The Talented Mr. Ripley" (we often made a show of introducing each other to our favorite movies via the two-dollar video place on Nassau), I was thinking of it as just a fluff movie until the very last part, when Ripley is forced to kill his lover to cover up his web of lies. I got an uncanny shiver just as the movie was ending, and I spent a long time in the bathroom trying to decide what to do, suddenly convinced that Anselm was a dangerous drifter, a charming psychotic. Even if he wasn't, the fact that I didn't know enough to prove otherwise had me highly agitated.

In the end, my weapon of choice was Tiger Balm. I pretended I had a neck ache and slathered the back of my neck and shoulders with the pungent ointment to keep him a certain distance away from me. By the next night, the fear had passed, or at least gone back underground.

Another time, we were hanging around my room, both involved in separate activities. I was sitting up reading in the very corner of the futon—where the two walls meet— and he was perched on the opposite corner. I remember he seemed less depressed that day—less heavy, slow energy and more spring in his step. He got up to fetch something from the living room. When he came back a second later, it was with quick, hard boot-steps, and a can of lighter fluid in his hand. He turned suddenly to face the bed, and I bolted off it just as quickly. By the time we caught each other's eye, he had opened his Zippo to refill it. I forced a laugh, I had to say it out loud—there was nothing else to do. "Sorry, honey, I thought you were about to set the bed on fire!"

28 December 2003

Anselm said the first time he came home from Ohio to see his mother, she didn't know who he was. It was right before Christmas. I think he came home with his friend Liza from Ann Arbor, the one who was crazy about gamelan music and Byzantine icons. They drove up in a clunker he'd bought in Cleveland, he had lost 53 pounds since the previous August, and his hair had grown past his shoulders. At first his mother mistook the two of them for "some East Coast do-gooders," and then she nearly fell over when she recognized his voice.

I find myself wondering if Anselm was intending to be real with me. It seemed at some points like the "promises" of his letters were getting more and more articulate, and even attuned to my heart's wishes, including things I hadn't spoken—his letters said everything I wanted to hear! While his actions were getting more and more hostile. The things he said, the small and constant ways he pushed me away, the things he didn't do, some things he did do. The gap between his love letters and his real self was getting wider, and then the letters stopped, and the depression worsened, so I started wondering all the time if he was just a scam artist.

And this is the feeling I'm left with—wondering what his real emotions were. Wondering if there was actual love that was sidetracked by a bad moment in his life. Or if I was being drained by some vampire who wanted to keep me in a state of constant questioning, of perpetual doubt. I felt bound in the space between his promises and his miseries. The thing was, I kept waiting for the him I recognized to come back for long enough to tell me what I should do with the him who became this needy, negative, suck-all creature.

I kept waiting for Anselm to protect me from himself. It disturbed me that he didn't apologize for himself at the very end—before or even after he left New York—but when I remembered the drunken moments when he *had* said "the right things," it disturbed me more.

29 December 2003

Anselm seemed to be enchanted with the Staten Island Ferry. He'd ridden it many times, surely it went with his love of rivers. I think it also appealed to his morbid side somehow, especially since he'd ridden it on September 11th, early in the morning. Before everything. He'd slept at Wendy's house on Staten Island the night before, his "depression friend" from Alabama, the one he can't always deal with, because she's heavy; depression is most of what they have in common. The one he met in the waiting room at Bellevue.

Then there was the Ferry crash. It happened, I think, right before Anselm left—mid-November. It was when Anselm had gotten very low, which seems obvious now, but at the time I was more aware of his false voice, the perpetual ploy for sympathy. I mean that I was constantly aware that he was asking for something from me when I thought it was his turn to give something to me. This was at a moment when I was consciously and intuitively trying to figure out if this person was good to be in a relationship with—was he good for me? Were we good for each other? Would the love between us be a fertile, growing thing— something to feed us both, heal us both? Or would we lean on each other to the point of discomfort, suffocation, in- stability, uselessness as a partnership?

But where was I? The day the Ferry crashed, the story

I came home to was: "I should have been on that ferry. I should have died on that ferry. I thought about taking the Ferry this afternoon." Inside, I rolled my eyes, for this was delivered in the fake voice, the whiny one. But was there supposed to be a concerned citizen in me that said, "Wake up! This guy is dangerously depressed! Get him some help before you're dragged down into the muck and can't see what's what!" Looking back, I can never tell.

It's been a long day because we got word this morning that Gran had a stroke in the middle of the night last night. So Mom was really sad and shaky and out of sorts all day, and I was sad for her. When I thought about Anselm today it was in imagining him dealing with the same thing. With his mother's mother getting sick, and dying. He was there in August helping her clear some things out of his grandmother's house, although it sounds like his mother and his aunt did most of the work.

What his grandmother left him was actually something of his grandfather's—a straight razor for shaving.

30 December 2003

At Union Station waiting for the train back to New York.

In the end, Anselm left the city just like he came—carrying one messenger bag, one suitcase, and one book of French deconstructionism for fending off the Bible-beaters on the long Greyhound ride west. We held each other after the loudspeaker announced the boarding for Pittsburgh, but not like at train stations in movies—no, it was just another gesture that was impossible for me to read one way or another. He said goodbye in a similarly ambiguous tone, too casual to signal a final chapter, too sullen to sound like a passionate parting.

I felt almost stupid that last day. I didn't know if Anselm was quitting me or New York City, and I didn't want to ask, I guess I felt like saying so was the very least he could do. I bought him some food for the bus and paid for a cab to Port Authority as if he still belonged to me, but when the bus finally backed away, I hurried home to Brooklyn and dragged our futon to the curb.

KAREN LILLIS was born in Washington, DC during the Vietnam War and has lived in Virginia, Texas, New York, Paris, and Pittsburgh. Her previous books of fiction include *The Second Elizabeth* (Six Gallery Press, 2009); *Magenta's Adventures Underground* (Words Like Kudzu Press, 2004; serialized in *New York Nights*, 2002-03); and *i, scorpion: foul belly-crawler of the desert* (Words Like Kudzu Press, 2000). In 2010 her prose was nominated for a Pushcart Prize. She is currently finishing her first book of nonfiction, *Bagging the Beats at Midnight: Confessions of a New York Bookstore Clerk*.

SPUYTEN DUYVIL

Meeting Eyes Bindery
Triton
Lithic Scatter

Made in the USA
Charleston, SC
18 March 2013